My Two Worlds

By GINGER GORDON

Photographs by

MARTHA COOPER

CLARION BOOKS

NEW YORK

CLARION BOOKS, a Houghton Mifflin Company imprint, 215 Park Avenue South, New York, NY 10003. Text copyright © 1993 by Ginger Gordon. Photographs copyright © 1993 by Martha Cooper. All rights reserved. For information about permission to reproduce selections from this book, write to Permissions, Houghton Mifflin Company, 215 Park Avenue South, New York, NY 10003. Printed in Singapore. Book design by Sylvia Frezzolini.

Library of Congress Cataloging-in-Publication Data Gordon, Ginger. My two worlds / by Ginger Gordon ; photographs by Martha Cooper. p. cm. Summary: Contrasts the two worlds of a six-year-old Dominican American girl who lives in New York City but speaks Spanish as her native language and frequently returns to her island home. ISBN 0-395-58704-2 1. Rodrigues, Kirsy—Juvenile literature. 2. Dominican Americans—New York (N.Y.)—Biography—Juvenile literature. 3. Dominican Americans—New York (N.Y.)—Social life and customs—Juvenile literature. 4. New York (N.Y.)—Biography—Juvenile literature. 5. New York (N.Y.)—Social life and customs—Juvenile literature. [1. Dominican Americans. 2. United States—Emigration and immigration. 3. Dominican Republic—Social life and customs.] I. Cooper, Martha, ill. II. Title. F128.9.D6G67 1993 974.7'1004687293'0092—dc20 [B] 92-39271 CIP AC

TWP 10 9 8 7 6 5 4 3 2 1

Kirsy's class

This book is dedicated to the students of P.S. 189

Thanks to the many people in New York and Puerto Plata who recognized the need for this book and helped make it possible. They include: James Norman, who brought us together and helped in so many ways; Dorothy Briley, our editor at Clarion Books; Elmer Sapadin, former principal of P.S. 189; and Rita Krinitz Gross, Kirsy's second-grade teacher. Special thanks to Kirsy's New York family: her mother and stepfather, Maria and Carmelo Albarracin; her brother and sister, Wendy and Cesar Elivo; and to her Puerto Plata family: her grandparents, Harry and Maria Luisa Gilbert; her cousins, Carolina and Shari Elivo; and the other relatives and friends whose faces brighten these pages. Thanks also to Kirsy's second-grade classmates: Merlin Bello, Albert Burgos, Miguel Casas, Paula Castillo, Tanya Clarke, Miguel Contreras, Michael Dilone, Orlando Feliz, Ileana Lagares, Fernando Lajora, Janeth Lopez, José Mateo, Victoria Matos, Jennifer Mendes, Wendy Ortiz, Zachary Ozuna, Maximo Paulino, Angel Payano, Yasser Pena, Diana Perez, Rosangela Rodriguez, Samuel Rodriguez, Sheryl Rodriguez, Mildred Rojas, Ursula Taveras. Special thanks to Kirsy Rodriguez, who did her part to make this book happen.

¡Hola!
I'm Kirsy Rodriguez.
My big sister Wendy
and I are going to the
Dominican Republic
for Christmas!

That's where the rest of my family is from. I am the only one born here. We all speak Spanish at home and English whenever we need to. I wish we could all go to Puerto Plata together. My mother and my stepfather, Carmelo, are busy with their jobs, and my brother Cesar has too much studying to do for college. From my grandparents' house I can run right down to the beach! I am so excited!

I love to shop for presents! It's going to be fun to give them out.
My mother and I don't want to forget anybody.

On the last day of school we had a great party. And I'm going to have my birthday party next week in Puerto Plata. I'll be eight years old.

School's out! Good-bye, everybody. See you next year. Puerto Plata, here I come!

On the plane, Wendy lets me have the window seat. I know what to look for—the Atlantic Ocean, Florida, the Bahamas, the islands in the West Indies, and finally, after about four hours, the beautiful beach of Puerto Plata.

We landed!
I change my watch so it's one hour later. Now I'm on Dominican time.

It's very hot here
in Puerto Plata!
Get me out of
these clothes!

It's great to be back. My grandpa built this house himself when he and Grandma got married. They've lived here for fifty years.

Everyone remembers me and is so friendly.

Here I can go outside
whenever I want.
Most of the time I
play with girlfriends.
We speak together in
Spanish because they
don't know English.

The neighborhood boys love to show off for us.

Kids in Puerto Plata work hard
helping their families.

YA LAS LOMAS Y LOS LLANOS
SE HAN VESTIDO DE MORAO

They bring home wood for cooking,   scrub the streets,

and carry water for drinking and washing.
Lots of kids go barefoot.

Many people get around on horses and
bikes and burros.

WOW! Uno, dos, tres, cuatro, cinco . . .
FIVE people on one little motor scooter!

My friend José helps out at the fire station. He's got a cute new puppy named Bomberito. That means "little fireman." I wish I could take him back to New York, but he probably wouldn't like being a city dog.

I like all the animals here. The rooster crowing outside my window wakes me up every morning. The little house lizards eat up lots of mosquitoes—but can you imagine house lizards in New York?

On Christmas morning we visit my cousins. They love the Monopoly game I brought them. We play until it's time for Christmas dinner.

My grandma has fixed
our favorite foods.
We stuff ourselves with
kibbe, pasteles, and
delicious, thick slices of
homemade bread.

The most fun comes after
dinner when we go outside to
dance in the street at night.
Tomorrow we'll go to Sosua.
It's the most beautiful beach in
the world.

The beach is hot and loaded
with tourists. There are so
many things to buy. We spend
almost all our pesos to have
our hair beaded and braided,
but it's worth it.

A visiting Italian family made a sand Ferrari and let me drive it.

That wave almost dunked me!
There's time for one last delicious
pineapple drink before we leave
the beach.

On the way home, I hear merengue music and start dancing.
I beg the musicians to come to my party tomorrow.

Today's my birthday. I'm eight years old. Everyone comes
to my party—even the beach musicians. We dance and dance.
Oh, what a merengue!

It's time to go home.
It makes me sad to say good-bye.
In less than four hours we'll be
back in New York City.

Mom,
I'm so glad to see you!

Oh, Carmelo!
Next time let's all go together.

I'm back on my own block. It looks beautiful.
Everything is covered with snow.

I'm going to get my sled. I hope it snows all winter.

Sometimes I wonder if
I'd rather live in the
Dominican Republic instead
of New York City.
Well, I don't know.
I'm glad I don't have
to choose—I belong to
both worlds and each is
a part of me.